W9-DHV-777

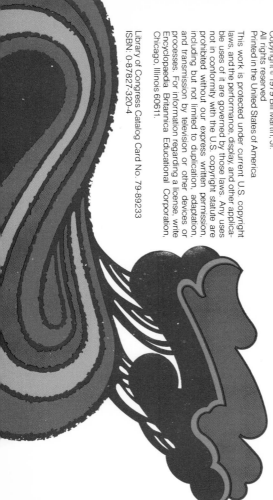

Bill Martin's
Little Woodland Books

A Read-Along Series

This work is protected under current U.S. copyright
laws, and the performance, display, and other applica-
ble uses of it are governed by those laws. Any uses
not in conformity with the U.S. copyright statute are
prohibited without our express written permission,
including but not limited to duplication, adaptation,
and transmission by television or other devices or
processes. For information regarding a license, write
Encyclopaedia Britannica Educational Corporation,
Chicago, Illinois 60611.

Library of Congress Catalog Card No. 79-89233
ISBN: 0-87827-320-4

The Wild Turkey and Her Poults

A Little Woodland Book
by Bill Martin Jr.

with watercolors by
Laura Cornell
handlettering by
Ray Barber

cassette recording
narrated by Bill Martin Jr.
with music by guitarist Al Caiola

EBE Encyclopaedia Britannica Educational Corporation
425 North Michigan Avenue. Chicago. Illinois 60611

A wild turkey steals away....

. . .steals away

from the turkey gobbler....

. . .steals away

from the other hens....

. . . steals away
from a spying 'possum . . . .

. . . steals away
from a crying crow . . .

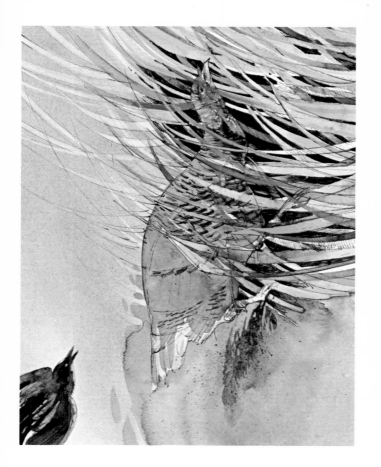

. . steals away
. . into a thicket
. . to build a secret nest . . . .

She fills the nest
with speckled eggs . . . .

. . . and sits on the nest

. . day after day . . .

. . to keep the eggs warm . . . .

Keeping the eggs safe and warm
becomes her aim in life. . . .
She never leaves her clutch of eggs
except for food and water. . . .

In 28 days...
the eggs hatch!

Immediately
the nesting hen
becomes a proud mother...
She leads her poults
away from the nest....

. . . on a dangerous journey
through the woods . . .
. . . clucking and beckoning
to keep her brood together . . .

At times of danger
she quickly hides her poults
from view. . . .
and calmly leads
the enemies astray

The poults are weak. . . .
and oh! so hungry. . . .
They eat all the berries
  . . . and seeds
  . . . and insects

they can find. . . .
and when their mother clucks
to tell them, "Here's some food! . . . .
they hurry to her side
and eat some more . . . .

At night
the tired little poults gather
under their mother's wings....
where they are warm....
and safe from harm....

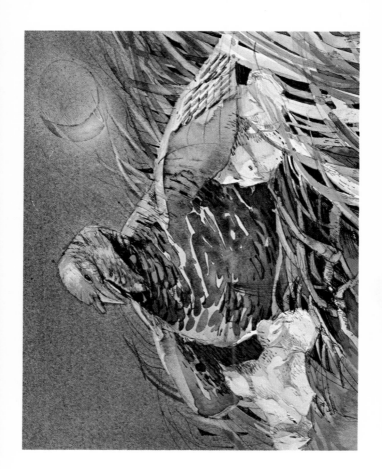

Two weeks later
the poults will be much stronger. . . .
. . . running like little bullets
through the thickets . . .
. . . crowding and shoving each other
to get at the food . . . .
. . . flying into the trees at night
to roost beside their mother. . . .
. . . but still snuggling
under her protecting wings . . . .